PUFFIN BOOKS

MOUSE TALES

Seven little mouse boys are tucked up snugly in bed.
But before they go to sleep, Papa has a story for each of
them.

What a mixture of mouse tales! A wishing well that says
'Ouch!', a dirty mouse's overflowing bath, pictures in
the clouds – each adventure has its own surprise!

MOUSE TALES

BY ARNOLD LOBEL

PUFFIN BOOKS

Puffin Books, Penguin Books Ltd, Harmondsworth, Middlesex, England
Viking Penguin Inc., 40 West 23rd Street, New York, New York 10010, U.S.A.
Penguin Books Australia Ltd, Ringwood, Victoria, Australia
Penguin Books Canada Ltd, 2801 John Street, Markham, Ontario, Canada L3R 1B4
Penguin Books (N.Z.) Ltd, 182–190 Wairau Road, Auckland 10, New Zealand

First published in Great Britain by World's Work Ltd, 1973
Published in Puffin Books 1985

Printed and bound in Great Britain by
William Clowes Limited, Beccles and London
Typeset in Times Roman

The I CAN READ books

CONTENTS

"Papa, we are all
in bed now,"
said the mouse boys.
"Please tell us a tale."
"I will do better than that,"
said Papa.
"I will tell you seven tales—
one for each of you—
if you promise
to go straight to sleep
when I have finished."
"Oh yes, we will,"
said the boys.

And Papa began. . .

THE WISHING WELL

A mouse once found

a wishing well.

"Now all my wishes

can come true!"

she cried.

She threw a penny

into the well

and made a wish.

"OUCH!"

said the wishing well.

The next day the mouse

came back to the well.

She threw a penny

into the well

and made a wish.

"OUCH!" said the well.

The next day

the mouse came back again.

She threw a penny

into the well.

"I wish this well

would not say ouch," she said.

"OUCH!" said the well.

"That hurts!"

"What shall I do?"

cried the mouse.

"My wishes

will never ever

come true this way!"

The mouse ran home.

She took the pillow

from her bed.

"This may help,"

said the mouse,

and she ran back

to the well.

The mouse threw the pillow

into the well.

Then she threw

a penny into the well

and made a wish.

"Ah. That feels

much better!"

said the well.

"Good!" said the mouse.

"Now I can start wishing."

After that day

the mouse made many wishes

by the well.

And every one of them

came true.

CLOUDS

A little mouse went for a walk
with his mother.
They went to the top of a hill
and looked at the sky.

"Look!" said Mother. "We can see pictures in the clouds."

The little mouse and his mother saw many pictures in the clouds. They saw a castle. . .

a rabbit. . .

a mouse.

"I am going to pick flowers,"
said Mother.
"I will stay here
and watch the clouds,"
said the little mouse.

The little mouse

saw a big cloud in the sky.

It grew bigger and bigger.

The cloud became a cat.

The cat came nearer and nearer

to the little mouse.

"Help!" shouted the little mouse,

and he ran to his mother.

"There is a big cat in the sky!"

cried the little mouse.

"I am afraid!"

Mother looked up at the sky.

"Do not be afraid," she said.

"See, the cat has turned back

into a cloud again."

The little mouse

saw that this was true,

and he felt better.

He helped his mother pick flowers,

but he did not look up at the sky

for the rest of the afternoon.

VERY TALL MOUSE
AND VERY SHORT MOUSE

Once there was a very tall mouse

and a very short mouse

who were good friends.

When they met

Very Tall Mouse would say,

"Hello, Very Short Mouse."

And Very Short Mouse would say,

"Hello, Very Tall Mouse."

The two friends would often

take walks together.

As they walked along

Very Tall Mouse would say,

"Hello birds."

And Very Short Mouse would say,

"Hello beetles."

When they

passed by a garden

Very Tall Mouse would say,

"Hello flowers."

And Very Short Mouse

would say,

"Hello roots."

When they passed by a house

Very Tall Mouse would say,

"Hello roof."

And Very Short Mouse

would say,

"Hello cellar."

One day the two mice

were caught in a storm.

Very Tall Mouse said,

"Hello raindrops."

And Very Short Mouse said,

"Hello puddles."

They ran indoors to get dry.

"Hello ceiling,"

said Very Tall Mouse.

"Hello floor,"

said Very Short Mouse.

Soon the storm was over.

The two friends

ran to the window.

Very Tall Mouse held

Very Short Mouse up to see.

"Hello rainbow!"

they both said together.

THE MOUSE AND THE WINDS

A mouse went out in his boat,

but there was no wind.

The boat did not move.

"Wind!" shouted the mouse.

"Come down and blow my boat

across this lake!"

"Here I am," said the west wind.

The west wind blew and blew.

The mouse and the boat

went up in the air. . .

and landed

on the roof of a house.

"Wind!" shouted the mouse.

"Come down and blow my boat

off this house!"

"Here I am," said the east wind.

The east wind blew and blew.

The mouse and the boat

and the house

went up in the air. . .

and landed on the top of a tree.

"Wind!" shouted the mouse.
"Come down and blow my boat
off this house
and off this tree!"

"Here I am,"

said the south wind.

The south wind blew and blew.

The mouse and the boat

and the house and the tree

went up in the air. . .

and landed

on the top of a mountain.

"Wind!" shouted the mouse.

"Come down and blow my boat

off this house

and off this tree

and off this mountain!"

"Here I am," said the north wind.

The north wind blew and blew.

The mouse and the boat

and the house and the tree

and the mountain

went up in the air...

and came down into the lake.

The mountain sank
and became an island.

The tree landed on the island
and burst into bloom.

The house landed next to the tree.

A lady looked out of a window

in the house

and said,

"What a nice place to live!"

And the mouse just sailed away.

THE JOURNEY

There was a mouse

who wanted to visit

his mother.

So he bought a car

and started to drive

to his mother's house.

He drove and

drove and drove

until the car fell apart.

But at the side of the road

there was a person

selling roller skates.

So the mouse bought

two roller skates

and put them on.

He rolled and rolled

and rolled

until the wheels fell off.

But at the side of the road

there was a person

who was selling boots.

So the mouse bought

two boots and put them on.

He tramped and tramped

 and tramped

until there were

big holes in the boots.

But at the side of the road

there was a person

who was selling gym shoes.

So the mouse bought

two gym shoes.

He put them on and ran

and ran and ran

until the gym shoes

were worn out.

So he took the gym shoes off

and walked and

walked and walked

until his feet hurt so much

that he could not go on.

But at the side of the road

there was a person

who was selling feet.

So the mouse took off his old feet

and put on new ones.

He ran the rest of the way

to his mother's house.

When he got there

his mother was glad to see him.

She hugged him and

kissed him,

and she said, "Hello, my son.

You are looking fine—

and what nice new feet

you have!"

THE OLD MOUSE

There was an old mouse

who went for a walk every day.

The old mouse

did not like children.

When he saw them on the street

he would shout,

"Go away, horrid things!"

One day the old mouse

was taking his walk.

All at once, his braces broke,

and his trousers fell down.

Some ladies came by.

"Help, help!" cried the old mouse.

But the ladies screamed,

"Your trousers have fallen down!"

And they ran away.

The old mouse ran home

and cried, "Help me!"

But his wife only said,

"You look silly

in your underwear,"

and gave him a bang on the head.

The old mouse began to cry.

Some children passed by.

"Poor old mouse," they said,

"we will help you.

Here is some chewing gum.

It will hold your trousers up

very well."

"Look!" cried the old mouse.

"My trousers are up!

This chewing gum is splendid.

These trousers will never

fall down again!"

Those trousers never did
fall down again.
And after that, the old mouse
was always kind to children
when he went for his walk.

THE BATH

There was once a mouse

who was dirty,

so he had a bath.

The water

filled up the bath.

But the mouse was still dirty,

so he let the water

run over onto the floor.

The water

filled up the bathroom.

But the mouse was still dirty,

so he let the water

run out of the window.

The water

filled up the street.

But the mouse was still dirty,

so he let the water
run into the house
next door.

The people
in the house next door
cried, "Turn off the water!
We have had
our bath today!"

But the mouse was still dirty,

so he let the water

run all over the whole town.

The people in the town cried,

"Turn off the water!

You are very clean now!"

The mouse said,

"Yes, you are right.

I am clean now."

So he turned off the water.

By then

the town was all wet.

But the mouse

did not care.

He rubbed himself

with a big towel

until he was very dry.

And then

he went straight to sleep.

"Is anybody awake?"

asked Papa.

There was no answer.

Seven small mice

were snoring.

"Good-night, my boys,"

said Papa,

"and sleep well.

I will see you all

in the morning."

The End